序　言

　　「中級英語檢定測驗」每一個高中生都要參加，不參加等於沒有高中畢業。將來沒有通過「中級英語檢定測驗」，就無法申請好的大學。未來的趨勢是，高中三年的教科書，只能當輔助閱讀資料，所有的高中生，都要積極準備此項檢定考試。

通過中級英語檢定考試，是高中生的目標。

　　「中級英語檢定測驗」初試部份，分為聽力測驗及閱讀能力測驗。其中，閱讀能力測驗包含詞彙與結構 15 題、段落填空 (即克漏字) 10 題、閱讀理解 (即閱讀測驗) 15 題。本書專門訓練同學的閱讀能力。

　　「中級英語檢定測驗」中的閱讀測驗，與「**大學學科能力測驗**」及「**指定科目考試**」的英文閱讀測驗相同。為了出題客觀，我們請多位老師命題，蒐集不同的資料，經過 1383 位同學實際測驗後，證明使用這本書，必可提升閱讀能力。

　　本書另附有「教師手冊」，每篇文章都有翻譯，每個句子都有文法分析，較難單字都有註解，節省讀者查字典的時間。學習出版公司的目標就是，每一本書，都要有詳詳細細的解說，不避重就輕。有看不懂的地方，是編者的責任。

　　歡迎讀者來信，或打電話給我們。有了你們的批評，我們才會更進步。

編者　謹識

本書製作過程

本書 Test 7 與 Test 8 由李麗莎老師命題，Test 11 至 Test 13 及 Test 21、23、26 由廖曄嵐老師命題，Test 16、19 及 Test 24 由唐慧莊老師命題，Test 1 至 Test 6，Test 9、10、14、15、18、20、22、25，及 Test 27 至 Test 50 由謝靜芳老師負責。全書完成後，先由命題老師校對完，又請 Andy Swarzman、Laura E. Stewart、Bill Allen 三位外籍老師詳細校對。

本書另附有教師手册，附有答案及詳解，售價 180 元。

再版的話

　　這一本閱讀測驗，經過1383位優秀的高二和高三同學，實際測驗過。我們以此試題，舉行「**全國高中英文閱讀測驗大賽**」，參加的同學包含：建中、北一女、師大附中、成功、中山、景美、延平、松山等學校同學。

　　同學在測驗之初，約在前10回，覺得做起來很吃力，答題速度又慢，但是，到了10幾回以後，很多同學就豁然開朗，答題速度加快，感覺到做起來輕鬆。連續做到30回以後，考過2小時之後，就開始覺得體力不支，頭昏眼花。一般同學拼命地寫，在150分鐘內，大約只能做到40回，只有少數幾位同學，能夠完全做完50回。

　　經過這次研究，我們覺得，本教材非常適合高一、高二、高三的學生使用。

　　高一：每10分鐘考1回，考後老師立刻講解。

　　高二：每15分鐘考2回，考後老師立刻講解。

　　高三：每30分鐘考5回，考後可讓同學自行看自修本。

　　只有在班上考試的時候，才有氣氛，使同學專心接受閱讀測驗的訓練。如果自己在家研讀，需要有很大的毅力。

劉　毅

TEST 1

Read the following passage, and choose the best answer for each question.

The girls arrived at the airport on time, but William did not. His plane was late and it was nearly one o'clock by the time he had taken care of all his business at the airport. Both he and the girls were quite hungry by that time, so they decided to eat lunch in the airport restaurant before they started home. Besides, they had a lot of things to talk about. William wanted to hear the latest news of his family and friends, and Helen and Betty wanted to ask questions about his work overseas. Helen was also interested in her brother's plans for the year ahead.

1. Which of the following statements is true?
   A. William went to the airport to meet his sisters who had returned from abroad.
   B. The plane was right on schedule.
   C. They had lunch before they left the airport for home.
   D. Helen was so hungry that she didn't care about William's future plans.

2. Which of the following statements is NOT true?
   A. The plane didn't arrive until one o'clock in the afternoon.
   B. The girls arrived at the airport earlier than William did.
   C. William had been away from home for some time.
   D. William had all his business settled at the airport before he ate lunch with Helen and Betty.

3. What do we know about William's work?

   A. He works in the airport.

   B. He is in business.

   C. He works in a foreign country.

   D. He works on a ship.

4. When did the girls arrive at the airport?

   A. They arrived before William did.

   B. They arrived at one o'clock.

   C. They arrived after lunch.

   D. They arrived late.

5. Why was William late?

   A. He missed his flight.

   B. There is a large time difference between his hometown
      and where he works.

   C. The airport was crowded.

   D. The flight was delayed.

TEST 2

Read the following passage, and choose the best answer for each question.

In order to qualify for a single room in a university dormitory, you must be a full-time student who has completed the necessary number of hours to be ranked as an upperclassman. Applicants for such university housing are required to submit completed applications to the Office of Student Housing at the beginning of the semester they are requesting such housing. Students will be notified regarding the status of their application by the sixth week of class. Private dorm rooms will be assigned to qualified students on a first-come, first-served basis.

1. According to this reading, in order for a student to get a single dormitory room he must _____
   A. be rich.
   B. be married.
   C. be a junior or senior.
   D. have superior grades.

2. When should a student apply for a single dormitory room?
   A. Before the semester begins.
   B. At the beginning of the semester.
   C. A few weeks after the semester begins.
   D. At the end of the preceding semester.

3. What is the main topic of this reading?

    A. Applying for a Dormitory Scholarship
    B. Applying to Share a Dormitory Room
    C. Regulations for University Admissions
    D. Regulations for Applying for a Private Dormitory Room

4. Why are the rooms assigned on a first-come, first-served basis?

    A. There are a limited number of single dormitory rooms available.
    B. There are enough dormitory rooms for all students.
    C. There are more single dormitory rooms than students who want them.
    D. There are not enough students who want single dormitory rooms.

5. Students will be informed of the status of their application _____

    A. at the end of the semester.
    B. one month before the semester ends.
    C. in the middle of the semester.
    D. one and a half months after the semester begins.

TEST 3

Read the following passage, and choose the best answer for each question.

The six year old is about the best example that can be found of that type of inquisitiveness that causes irritated adults to exclaim, "Curiosity killed the cat." To him, the world is a fascinating place to be explored thoroughly, and it is constantly expanding through new experiences, which bring many eager questions from members of any group of first graders, as each one tries to figure out his place within the family, the school, and the community. There are adults who find it quite annoying to be presented with such inquisitiveness. But this is no purposeless prying, no idle curiosity! It is that quality, characteristic of the successful adult, inherent in the good citizen — intellectual curiosity.

1. According to this passage, inquisitiveness is _____
    A. an annoying quality.
    B. only found in the six year olds.
    C. killing the cat.
    D. characteristic of the successful adult.

2. The author's attitude in this passage toward children is one of _____
    A. despair.
    B. confidence.
    C. sharp criticism.
    D. indifference.

3. "Curiosity killed the cat" as used in this passage probably means to suggest that an inquisitive person is likely to _____

   A. succeed.
   B. suffer injury or harm.
   C. raise many eager questions.
   D. become a good citizen.

4. A word that could meaningfully replace "prying" as used in this passage is _____

   A. exploring.
   B. expanding.
   C. support.
   D. fascination.

5. In writing this passage, the author's purpose is _____

   A. to defend the inquisitiveness of the child.
   B. to criticize such inquisitiveness.
   C. to discuss the pros and cons of curiosity.
   D. to report the result of a study on curiosity.

TEST 4

Read the following passage, and choose the best answer for each question.

Omar's army had been victorious over the Persian forces. The conquered chieftain was taken prisoner and condemned to death. As a last boon he asked for a cup of wine. It was brought to him. Seeing that he hesitated to raise it to his lips, Omar assured him that neither was the wine poisoned, nor was there anyone there who would kill him while he drank. Omar added that he gave his word as a prince and a soldier that his captive's life was safe until he had drunk the last drop of wine. At these words, the Persian poured the wine upon the ground and demanded that Omar keep his promise. In spite of the angry protests of his followers, Omar kept his word and allowed his prisoner to go free.

1. Omar assured the chieftain that —————
    A. he would be killed if he drank the wine.
    B. probably no poison had been dissolved in the wine.
    C. he was safe until he had drunk the last drop of wine.
    D. he was a prince and a soldier.

2. The chieftain poured the wine upon the ground —————
    A. after he had asked Omar to keep his promise.
    B. after he had drunk a little.
    C. immediately after Omar had given his word.
    D. immediately after he had hesitated.

3. The chieftain poured the wine because ――――――

    A. he wanted to escape.

    B. he wanted to be given his freedom.

    C. he wanted to be alone.

    D. he was afraid of the angry protests of Omar's followers.

4. The conquered chieftain showed ――――――

    A. cleverness.

    B. kindness.

    C. a sense of honor.

    D. bravery.

5. The best title for this selection is ――――――

    A. Omar's Victory.

    B. An Unworthy Chieftain.

    C. The Wine of Promise.

    D. Omar's Honor.

TEST 5

Refer to the following timetable:

Train	Lv. Boston	Ar. Midway	Ar. New York
	Timetable		
504	5:10 AM Ex. Sun	7:00 AM	10:45 AM
131	7:10 AM Daily	9:00 AM	12:45 PM
62	9:10 AM Ex. Sat. & Sun.	11:00 AM	2:45 PM
797	10:00 AM Ex. Hol.	11:45 AM	......
234	1:15 PM Daily	3:15 PM	5:45 PM
501	3:40 PM Ex. Hol.	5:40 PM	8:15 PM
236	5:20 PM Daily	7:20 PM	9:55 PM

1. How many times a week does the 9:10 AM train arrive in New York from Boston?

   A. 6 times.   B. 5 times.
   C. 7 times.   D. 2 times.

2. What is the shortest elapsed time between Boston and New York?

   A. 5 hours, 35 minutes.
   B. 5 hours, 5 minutes.
   C. 4 hours, 30 minutes.
   D. 4 hours, 25 minutes.

3. You have a luncheon date at Midway on Saturday. What time must you leave Boston in order not to be late?

    A. 5:00 AM.   B. 7:10 AM.

    C. 9:10 AM.   D. 10:00 AM.

4. If you need to leave Boston by 1:30 pm, and arrive in New York before 9:00 pm, which train do you need to take?

    A. 501   B. 62

    C. 234   D. 797

5. If you need to arrive in New York every day after 1:00 pm, how many different trains can you take?

    A. 1   B. 3

    C. 2   D. 4

TEST 6

Read the following passage, and choose the best answer for each question.

High in the Swiss Alps many years ago there lived a lonely shepherd boy who longed for a friend to share his evenings. One night he saw three wrinkled old men each holding a glass. The first said, "Drink this liquid and you shall be victorious in battle."

The second one said, "Drink this liquid and you shall have countless riches."

The last man said, "I offer you the happiness of music — the horn."

The boy chose the third glass. Next day he came upon a great horn, ten feet in length. When he put his lips to it, a beautiful melody floated across the valley. He had found a friend.

So goes the legend of the horn. Known in the ninth century, the horn was used by herdsmen to call cattle, for the deep tones echoed across the mountainsides. And even today, on a quiet summer evening, its music can be heard floating among the peaks.

1. What is the topic of this reading?
   A. The Hobbies of Shepherd Boys
   B. The Legend of the Horn
   C. The History of the Swiss Alps
   D. The Dreams of Shepherd Boys

2. What detail about the shepherd boy does this reading tell us?

    A. He has a lonely job.

    B. His age.

    C. His name.

    D. His singing ability.

3. Why did the boy choose to drink the glass offered by the last old man?

    A. The boy liked the old man.

    B. The boy didn't like the other old men.

    C. The boy loved music.

    D. The boy was thirsty.

4. After the shepherd boy found the horn, he discovered it was _____

    A. stolen from someone else.

    B. very easy to carry with him.

    C. impossible to play.

    D. like having a new friend.

5. Today the horn is heard in the Swiss Alps _____

    A. in the spring.   B. in the summer.

    C. in the autumn.   D. in the winter.

TEST 7

Read the following passage, and choose the best answer for each question.

It is against this background of corruption, revolution, hypocrisy, and greed that the Soong legend begins.

Few families since the Borgias have played such a disturbing role in human destiny. For nearly a century they were key players in events that shaped the history of Asia and the world. Members of the Soong clan became household names — Dr. Sun Yat-sen, Madame Chiang Kai-shek, Generalissimo Chiang, Madame Sun. Others served as China's prime ministers, foreign ministers, finance ministers. They amassed some of the greatest fortunes of the age; T.V. Soong may have been the richest man on earth.

1. Without the unstable situation in China, the Soongs would probably —————
   A. never have played so important a role in China and the world.
   B. have achieved more success.
   C. have become more famous for their dynasty.
   D. have gone anywhere.

2. From the passage, we know that —————
   A. the Borgias can't have affected history very much.
   B. the Soong family were not as important and distinguished as the Borgias.
   C. only a few families have been as outstanding as the Soong family and the Borgias.
   D. most families can be as remarkable as the Soongs and the Borgias.

3. According to what is mentioned in the passage, which one is not true?

    A. Members of the Soong clan were either famous or rich.
    B. Many families can be compared with the Soongs.
    C. Few families have been so rich and unusual as the Soongs.
    D. Many members of the Soong family have served high positions.

4. From which phrase can we infer that the writer doesn't think highly of the Soongs?

    A. the greatest fortunes
    B. the richest man
    C. household names
    D. a disturbing role

5. Maybe we can say ――――――

    A. the Soong family played a minor role in Asian history.
    B. Asia has been prosperous because of the Soongs.
    C. no corruption, no Soong success.
    D. without a revolution, there wouldn't be any corruption.

TEST 8

Read the following passage, and choose the best answer for each question.

Constant change is an integral part of the Communist philosophy. For the entire thirty-eight years of Communist rule in China, the Party's policy has swung like a pendulum from left to right and back again without stop. Unless and until a political system rooted in law, rather than personal power, is firmly established in China, the road to the future will always be full of twists and turns. The wanton use of personal power such as Mao wielded during the Cultural Revolution may yet turn back the clock. Factional struggle for power among the new leaders is almost a certainty, though there will be an interval of superficial unity while each man consolidates his position. The Chinese people will continue to stand on the sidelines, allowed to speak only with an affirmative voice.

1. The Communist Party ――――――
   A. has tried hard to stop their pendulum work.
   B. seems to be in full swing.
   C. is always changing their policy.
   D. wants to adhere to steady measures.

2. Based on this passage, we see that ――――――
   A. the author believes policy should change.
   B. the author hopes for simple unity.
   C. the writer approves of the way Mao ruled.
   D. the writer prefers a political system rooted in law.

3. According to this passage, we can conclude ——————

   A. new leaders should strive for power.

   B. the road to the future should be steady and predictable.

   C. the Chinese should only be allowed to speak well of the authorities.

   D. the Chinese people should not take part in making the policy of the government.

4. "Superficial " is synonymous with ——————

   A. shallow.   B. wanton.

   C. artificial.   D. superb.

5. The writer of this passage ——————

   A. wishes each leader to strengthen his position.

   B. is opposed to faction fighting.

   C. thinks that Mao had the power and used it in a proper way and wishes that Mao could come back to rule China.

   D. wants the Chinese people to show their approval of the policy unanimously.

TEST 9

Read the following passage, and choose the best answer for each question.

Specialists in marketing have studied how to make people buy more food in a supermarket. They do all kinds of things that you do not even notice. For example, the simple, ordinary food that everybody must buy, like bread, milk, flour, and vegetable oil, is spread all over the store. You have to walk by all the more interesting — and more expensive — things in order to find what you need. The more expensive food is in packages with brightly-colored pictures. This food is placed at eye level so you see it and want to buy it. The things that you have to buy anyway are usually located on a higher or lower shelf. However, candy and other things that children like are on lower shelves. One study showed that when a supermarket moved four products from floor to eye level, it sold 78 percent more.

1. In a supermarket the simple and ordinary food is —————
   A. placed at eye level.
   B. placed on a higher shelf.
   C. located on a lower shelf.
   D. spread all over the store.

2. Packages that have brightly-colored pictures are —————
   A. the more expensive food.
   B. cheap food.
   C. ordinary food.
   D. children's food.

3. Children can find candy and other things they like _____

    A. on lower shelves.

    B. on higher shelves.

    C. on lower and higher shelves.

    D. at eye level.

4. A supermarket can increase sales by _____

    A. selling more expensive products.

    B. moving products from floor to eye level.

    C. packing goods brightly.

    D. cheating customers.

5. Specialists in marketing know a lot about _____

    A. consumer psychology.

    B. consumers' eyesight.

    C. consumers' purchasing power.

    D. the art of packaging.

TEST 10

Refer to the following telephone listing:

Lads and Lassies Play School
    2902 N.W. 22nd Place   375-7742

Land Clearing Service
    RFD Millville   462-1606

Lannon's Real Estate
    905 S.E. 2nd Terrace   372-9636

Larry's Pools Inc.
    4100 Oak Street   377-4276

London Recreation Club
    214 S. 33rd Drive   378-8432

1. Which number would you call if you wanted to play tennis?

    A. 372-9636.   B. 375-7742.
    C. 378-8432.   D. 377-4276.

2. Which number would you call if you were looking for a house or an apartment?

    A. 375-7742.   B. 372-9636.
    C. 462-1606.   D. 378-8432.

3. Which number would you call to find a place to leave your children?
   A. 378-8432.   B. 375-7742.
   C. 377-4276.   D. 462-1606.

4. Which number is most likely not a local number?
   A. 375-7742.   B. 378-8432.
   C. 462-1606.   D. 372-9636.

5. Which number would you call for swimming equipment?
   A. 375-7742.   B. 378-8432.
   C. 377-4276.   D. 372-9636.

TEST 11

Read the following passage, and choose the best answer for each question.

Why do people take part in such a risky activity as bungee jumping? They jump from a high place (perhaps a bridge or a hot-air balloon) 200 meters above the ground with an elastic rope tied to their ankles. According to psychologists, it is because life in modern societies has become safe and boring. Not very long ago, people's lives were constantly under threat. They had to go out and hunt for food, diseases could not easily be cured, and life was a continuous battle for survival. Nowadays, according to many people, life offers little excitement. They live and work in comparatively safe environments; they buy food in shops; and there are doctors and hospitals to look after them if they become ill. The answer for some of these people is to seek danger in activities such as bungee jumping.

1. In bungee jumping, people —————
   A. jump as high as they can.
   B. slide down a rope to the ground.
   C. attach a rope and fall to the ground.
   D. fall towards the ground without a rope.

2. People probably take part in dangerous sports nowadays because —————
   A. they have a lot of free time.
   B. they can go to hospital if they are injured.
   C. their lives lack excitement.
   D. they no longer need to hunt for food.

3. The place which is not suitable for bungee jumping is ———

    A. a bridge two hundred meters high.

    B. a cliff.

    C. a hot-air balloon.

    D. a five-story building.

4. If we were living in ancient times now, ————

    A. we would have to hunt for food.

    B. we could buy food in shops.

    C. we would have doctors to look after our health.

    D. we would have little excitement.

5. Life in the past was basically a continuous battle for ————

    A. fame.   B. wealth.

    C. survival.   D. power.

TEST 12

Read the following passage, and choose the best answer for each question.

The executive branch of the American government puts the country's laws into effect. The president of the United States is a member of the executive branch. The president must be at least 35 years old, and be a natural citizen of the United States. In addition, he must have lived in the United States for at least 14 years, and be a civilian. The president is elected every four years and can not serve more than two terms in a row. The vice president acts as president of the Senate. When the president receives a bill from Congress, he must sign it in order for it to become a law. However, if he disagrees with the law, he can veto, or reject, it. The president can also ask the Congress to declare war. He also appoints the justices to the Supreme Court. He must do his job according to the Constitution, or he may be impeached, that is, charged with a crime by Congress. The executive branch is a very important part of the U.S. government and must work with the other two branches, i.e., the judicial branch and the legislative branch, according to the Constitution.

1. The president of the United States must be _____
   A. no more than 35.
   B. under 35.
   C. at least 35.
   D. over 49.

2. In the States, the presidential election takes place ——————

    A. every six years.

    B. every five years.

    C. every four years.

    D. every other year.

3. According to the Constitution, the Congress can ——————

    A. impeach the president if he acts against the law.

    B. appoint the justices to the Supreme Court.

    C. act as the president of the Senate.

    D. not declare war against another country.

4. The president of the United States must be ——————

    A. a naturalized citizen.

    B. a natural citizen.

    C. a civilized person.

    D. a judge.

5. The American government is mainly made up of ——————

    A. two branches.

    B. three branches.

    C. four branches.

    D. five branches.

TEST 13

Read the following passage, and choose the best answer for each question.

According to news reports, drunk driving has become increasingly common over the past few years. It is time for the authorities to assume a truly tough stance toward this dangerous act. Driving under the influence of alcohol is even more dangerous than speeding and running a red light. A driver who is drunk can lose control of his or her vehicle suddenly and hit any pedestrians and automobiles on the road that happen to be in his path, and the result is usually a fatal tragedy. Car ownership has increased rapidly in recent years because of elevated living standards. And drinking is an addiction among a growing number of the island's residents. These trends have combined to make drunk driving widespread. The only effective way to reduce drunk driving is to make the laws stiffer and enforce them more strictly.

1. Drunk driving usually results in _____
   A. comedy.
   B. tragedy.
   C. law-abiding acts.
   D. control of one's vehicle.

2. A drunken driver is unable to keep his car under control
   because of the influence of _____
      A. pedestrians.   B. alcohol.
      C. laws.   D. reports.

3. The rise of living standards has enabled more and more
   people to _____
      A. run a red light.
      B. be addicted to drunk driving.
      C. own private cars.
      D. control their vehicles well.

4. The only effective way to reduce drunk driving is to
   _____
      A. take weak measures against drunken drivers.
      B. enforce laws more strictly.
      C. build better roads.
      D. stop stores from selling wines.

5. In comparison with speeding and running a red light,
   drunk driving _____
      A. requires more driving skills.
      B. is a more dangerous act.
      C. is scarcely seen.
      D. does not endanger pedestrians.

TEST 14

Read the following passage, and choose the best answer for each question.

I am more of a host than a guest. I like people to stay with me but do not much care for staying with them, and usually say I am too busy. The only people we ask to stay with us are people we like — I do not believe in business hospitality, which has the seed of corruption in it — and every Friday I work in a pleasant glow just because I know some nice people are coming down by the last train. I am genuinely glad to see them. But I suspect that I am still more delighted when they go, and the house is ours again.

1. Often on Fridays, the writer will be _____
    A. anticipating the arrival of his guests.
    B. ready to retire for the weekend.
    C. sending out invitations.
    D. prepared to start working again.

2. All things considered, the writer _____
    A. enjoys the company of business associates more than personal friends.
    B. is a great host, to whose parties many celebrities come.
    C. would rather be left alone to the peace and quiet of his home.
    D. might yet prove himself to be a better guest than a generous host.

3. When turning down a friend's invitation, the writer will say,
   _____

   A. "I am more of a host."
   B. "I am not much of a guest."
   C. "I do not much care."
   D. "My time is fully employed."

4. The writer does not consider business entertainment worth
   his while because _____
   A. he does not like his business friends.
   B. he does not think they are pleasant companions.
   C. he suspects there is a dishonest motive.
   D. business friends are mostly corrupt.

5. The writer probably lives _____
   A. in the city.
   B. in the country.
   C. in a foreign country.
   D. within a short walk from his office.

TEST 15

Read the following passage, and choose the best answer for each question.

POPULATION CHANGES —
RECENT CENSUS STATISTICS

	1990	2000
Oak Hill	 34,510	34,265
Holly	 19,451	10,900
Avondale	 6,782	15,943
Beechwood	 7,569	7,620
Lakeside	 1,243	998

1. Which of the following cities increased its population considerably during the ten-year period?

   A. Avondale.   B. Beechwood.

   C. Oak Hill.   D. Holly.

2. Which city showed the most appreciable decrease in population in the ten-year period?

   A. Beechwood.   B. Oak Hill.

   C. Holly.   D. Lakeside.

3. Which city's population decreased by the smallest percentage?

    A. Holly.
    B. Lakeside.
    C. Beechwood.
    D. Oak Hill.

4. Which city had no population increase or decrease?

    A. Oak Hill.
    B. Lakeside.
    C. Beechwood.
    D. None of the above.

5. If someone wants to start his own service business, which city will probably offer the best opportunities for success?

    A. Oak Hill.
    B. Beechwood.
    C. Holly.
    D. Lakeside.

TEST 16

Read the following passage, and choose the best answer for each question.

The aye-aye is a rainforest animal. It eats insects which live under the bark of trees. It has very good ears. It's capable of hearing the slightest sound. It puts its ear next to the bark of a tree and listens for signs of movement. Then it quickly bites a hole in the bark and puts its middle finger into the hole to pull out the insect. It also uses its middle finger for combing its hair.

It lives only in Madagascar. It sleeps during the day and is active at night. It often hangs upside down from branches. And the strong claws on its feet are used as hooks. It is called "aye-aye" after the strange noises it makes, which are blown through its nose. The island people are frightened of the noises.

1. The aye-aye feeds on ―――――
   A. barks.   B. fruit.
   C. insects.   D. leaves.

2. The aye-aye lives in ―――――
   A. trees.   B. caves.
   C. holes.   D. many places.

3. The aye-aye gets its food with ―――――

    A. its long tongue.

    B. its middle finger.

    C. the claws on its feet.

    D. hooks.

4. Which statement about the aye-aye is wrong?

    A. It sleeps during the day and is active at night.

    B. It is called "aye-aye" because it makes strange noises "aye-aye".

    C. The strange noises it makes are from its nose.

    D. It has very good eyes so that it is active at night.

5. Madagascar is ―――――

    A. a rainforest.   B. a kind of tree.

    C. an island.   D. an insect.

TEST 17

Read the following passage, and choose the best answer for each question.

Brazilian food is like Brazil itself. It's a rich mixture of many things from many places. Some dishes are like Portuguese dishes because many Portuguese people went to live in Brazil. Other dishes are not like any European dishes. The flavors are special to Brazil. Brazilian cooks are lucky. They can get excellent fish from the ocean, and good meat from the farms. And they can get all kinds of tropical fruits and vegetables, which give Brazilian dishes their special delicious taste. Brazil is a large country. Each area has its own history and traditions, and so has its own way of cooking. If you are in Rio de Janeiro, you should try the "feijoada," a very rich mixture of different meats with black beans. Brazilians usually eat it on the weekend. It's not a dish to eat in a hurry.

1. The article is about _____
   A. Brazilian cooks.
   B. Brazil.
   C. Brazilian food.
   D. Brazilian history.

2. Brazilian food _____
   A. is all the same.
   B. is all like Portuguese food.
   C. is a mixture of different foods.
   D. has no special flavors.

3. The special taste of Brazilian food comes from —————

    A. the ocean.

    B. the farms.

    C. tropical fruits and vegetables.

    D. Portugal.

4. "Feijoada" is a dish very special to —————

    A. Europe.

    B. Portugal.

    C. Brazil.

    D. Rio de Janeiro.

5. Brazilians usually eat "feijoada" —————

    A. on holidays.

    B. on the weekend.

    C. in a hurry.

    D. at the beach.

TEST 18

Read the following passage, and choose the best answer for each question.

Recently in Greece many parents complained about the difficult homework which teachers gave to their children. The parents said most of the homework was a waste of time, and they wanted to stop it. Spain and Turkey are two countries which stopped homework recently. In Denmark, Germany and several other countries in Europe, teachers cannot set homework on weekends. In Holland, teachers allow pupils to stay at school to do their homework. The children are free to help one another. Similar arrangements also exist in some British schools.

Most parents agree that homework is unfair. A pupil who can do his homework in a quiet and comfortable room is in a much better position than a pupil who does his homework in a small, noisy room with the television on. Some parents help their children with their homework, while others don't.

1. Greek parents complained about —————
   A. the strict teachers.
   B. the unfair teachers.
   C. too much homework.
   D. the difficult homework.

2. In —————, homework has been stopped.
   A. Greece   B. Turkey
   C. Denmark   D. Britain

3. In ——————, teachers can't set homework at weekends.

    A. Greece   B. Holland

    C. Britain   D. Germany

4. In Holland, ——————

    A. children can do homework at school.

    B. children have to do homework without others' help.

    C. children have less homework on weekends.

    D. parents want to stop children's homework.

5. Most parents think homework unfair because ——————

    A. it is a waste of time.

    B. all the children do their homework with the television on.

    C. some parents help their children with their homework, but others don't.

    D. some homework is easy, while some is difficult.

TEST 19

Read the following passage, and choose the best answer for each question.

The native people of North America made general use of body painting. When warriors prepared for battle, they would paint themselves with bold designs. They concentrated on their faces which were decorated with red stripes, black masks or white circles around the eyes. These designs made the warrior look fierce and aggressive. Other peoples also used war paint. When the Romans invaded Britain, they found that the Ancient Britons painted themselves with blue paint called woad before going into battle.

Body painting can be used for occasions other than battles. The aboriginal peoples of Australia often decorate their bodies with bold white markings for a corroboree. It is a special meeting at which men dance and sing.

1. The best title for this article is —————
   A. battle and body painting.
   B. war paint.
   C. body painting.
   D. ways of body decoration.

2. There were ————— around the eyes of the native warriors of North America.
   A. red stripes   B. black masks
   C. white circles   D. blue woad

3. The bold designs focused on the ——————— of the native warriors of North America.

   A. bodies   B. faces
   C. arms and legs   D. eyes

4. ——————— wore "woad" for battle.

   A. The Ancient Britons
   B. The Romans
   C. Australian aboriginal peoples
   D. The native people of North America

5. A corroboree is a special occasion on which men ———————

   A. look fierce.
   B. must be bold.
   C. dance and eat.
   D. sing and dance.

TEST 20

Refer to the following textbook index:

1. On which of the pages of the textbook would one look to find the cases of arbitration and mediation?

   A. 83.   B. 94.
   C. 154.   D. 519.

2. Which of the following pages would most likely contain a series of problems regarding exclusive control of a commodity or service?

   A. 94-230.   B. 154-156.
   C. 494.   D. 519.

3. On which of the pages would one find the information with regard to the stockholders of a company?

   A. 83.   B. 94-230.
   C. 314-316.   D. 494.

4. In which section of the index would one find information about a sharp and sudden rise of prices resulting from a too great expansion in paper money or bank credit?

   A. Assets.
   B. Investment and taxation.
   C. Monopoly and antitrust.
   D. Unemployment and inflation.

5. Under which heading would one find information on payments made by public corporations to its shareholders?

   A. Assets.
   B. Investment and taxation.
   C. Dividends.
   D. Monopoly and antitrust.

TEST 21

Read the following passage, and choose the best answer for each question.

Traditional festivals are important events in the life of every Chinese, beginning right from childhood. Festivals such as Chinese New Year, the Dragon Boat Festival, the Mid-Autumn Festival, and the Winter Solstice are more or less evenly distributed across the four seasons. In China's traditional agricultural society, festivals served to mark the passing of time. Lifestyles of the people of the Republic of China today have undeniably changed a great deal since those times, and people now function according to a different concept of time, but the importance of traditional festivals in their lives has not faded.

1. Before the Chinese New Year, the last festival we Chinese here celebrate is _____
   A. the Mid-Autumn Festival.
   B. the Dragon Boat Festival.
   C. the Winter Solstice.
   D. the Ghost Festival.

2. With the passing of time, people's lifestyles in Taiwan have _____
   A. remained the same.
   B. changed a lot.
   C. changed little.
   D. appeared strange.

3. The importance of traditional festivals in the life of every
   Chinese can not be —————

      A. seen.   B. realized.

      C. overemphasized.   D. distributed.

4. We Chinese people eat mooncakes on —————

      A. the Dragon Boat Festival.

      B. the Mid-Autumn Festival.

      C. the Winter Solstice.

      D. the Lantern Festival.

5. Today, Taiwan's society has changed into —————

      A. an industrial one.

      B. an agricultural one.

      C. an ancient one.

      D. an eventful one.

TEST 22

Read the following passage, and choose the best answer for each question.

The early adolescent seems to be in a state that is difficult for most adults to understand. Parents, in particular, are often at a loss for how to deal with someone they thought they knew but who now seems changed. Changeability and contradiction are characteristic of youngsters during this time. They want to be independent and reject parental control, appearing at times extremely rebellious. At the same time they conform almost sheepishly to their peers' standards of dress, music, and behavior. They seem to be completely self-centered and materialistic one moment, then suddenly shift to an altruistic giving of themselves in the service of some social or political cause. They can be extremely inconsiderate and tactless one day, remarkably sensitive the next. Their moods can change within minutes from being on top of the world to feeling that everything is hopeless. Consistency is totally missing, and these rapid shifts and contradictions seem hard to comprehend.

1. Parents find adolescents hard to understand because
   _____

   A. they are always self-centered and inconsiderate.
   B. they want to be independent.
   C. the parents feel loss.
   D. they are inconsistent.

2. The state of adolescence is —————

   A. sheepish.   B. consistent.
   C. changeable.   D. angry.

3. The author probably thinks —————

   A. adolescence is a difficult period.
   B. adolescents are bad.
   C. adolescents are treated too softly in today's society.
   D. parents should be more strict with their adolescent
      children.

4. Sometimes youngsters devote themselves to the service of
   some social or political cause because they are —————

   A. altruistic.   B. materialistic.
   C. sensitive.   D. tactless.

5. The author's tone in this passage is —————

   A. contradictory.   B. confused.
   C. understanding.   D. apologetic.

TEST 23

Read the following passage, and choose the best answer for each question.

The human race is only one small species of beings in the living world; many other groups exist among the creatures on this planet. However, human beings have a great influence on the rest of the world. People change the environment by building cities where forests once stood. People affect the water supply by using water for industry and agriculture. People affect weather conditions by increasing the amount of water in the air; when open land is changed into farms, the humidity of the atmosphere in that area increases because of the increased vegetation. Human beings change the air by adding pollutants like smoke from factories and fumes from automobile motors. Thus, it can be said that the human species changes the world through its actions and by its habits. People, in other words, are interfering with nature.

1. The main idea of this passage is to tell the reader that _____
   A. human beings need to grow food.
   B. human beings pollute the environment.
   C. people's habits affect the world.
   D. people should stop living in cities.

2. An increasing number of plants in a certain area will affect _____

    A. people's activities.

    B. the cultivation of land.

    C. the development of industry and agriculture.

    D. the humidity of the atmosphere.

3. On this planet, the Earth, live _____

    A. only the human race.

    B. only the wild animals.

    C. a small species of beings.

    D. all sorts of creatures.

4. The effect human actions and habits have on the rest of the world is _____

    A. beneficial.   B. healthy.

    C. far-reaching.   D. unknown.

5. Turning forests into building sites will _____

    A. improve the quality of air.

    B. change the face of the environment.

    C. reduce the number of farms.

    D. increase employment opportunities.

TEST 24

Read the following passage, and choose the best answer for each question.

Advertising is the difficult business of bringing information to great numbers of people. The purpose of an ad is to make people respond — to make them react to an idea, such as helping to prevent forest fires, or to make them want to buy a certain product or service.

At the beginning of the 20th century, advertising was described as "salesmanship in print." If this definition were expanded to include radio, television, and the Internet, it would still stand today. The most effective way to sell something is through person-to-person contact. But the cost is high. Because it takes a great deal of time, it increases the cost of the product or service. However, advertising distributes the selling message to many people at one time.

1. This article is mainly about _____
   A. the definition of advertising.
   B. advertising at the beginning of the 20th century.
   C. why advertising is a difficult business.
   D. the most effective way of selling a certain product.

2. According to this article, the most effective way to sell something is _____
   A. through advertising.
   B. through direct contact.
   C. through mail order.
   D. putting an ad on the Internet.

3. The cost of selling through advertising is ——————— that of person-to-person selling.

   A. higher than
   B. lower than
   C. the same as
   D. not so low as

4. "Salesmanship in print" refers to selling by putting ads
   ———————

   A. on television.
   B. on the radio.
   C. in the newspaper.
   D. on the Internet.

5. From this article, we have learned that ———————

   A. it is easy to make people buy something by advertising it.
   B. the purpose of an ad is only to make people buy a product or service.
   C. advertising brings the selling message to many people at one time, so it is more effective than person-to-person selling.
   D. the cost of person-to-person selling is high because it takes lots of time.

TEST 25

Read the following passage, and choose the best answer for each question.

MARKHAM PLUMBING & HEATING

Since 1935

Plumbing and Heating Installation

LARGE OR SMALL REPAIRS

RESIDENTIAL · COMMERCIAL

FREE ESTIMATES

N. J. State License # 4807

24 Hour 7 Day Service

228 - 4495

461 GORDON WAY

HARRINGTON

---

1. What service is offered free by Markham Plumbing & Heating?

   A. Installation.
   B. State licensing.
   C. Cost estimates.
   D. Large or small repairs.

2. In the ad, which of the following indicates that Markham Plumbing & Heating has been in business for a long time?
   A. "Since 1935"
   B. "N.J. State License # 4807"
   C. "24 Hour 7 Day Service"
   D. "Plumbing and Heating Installation"

3. For which of the following problems would one call
   Markham Plumbing & Heating?

   A. A leak in the roof.
   B. A gas leak in the refrigerator.
   C. A short circuit in a wall plug that causes all the lights
      to go out.
   D. A broken bathroom pipe that is leaking water all
      over the floor.

4. The words "Residential · Commercial" in the ad indicate
   that Markham Plumbing & Heating —————

   A. is licensed as a commercial establishment to do work
      for private residences.
   B. is a profit-making business with a plumber always
   in residence.
   C. operates from a private home but makes commercial
      repairs.
   D. does work for private homes as well as for business.

5. What information certifies the company in the State
   of N.J.?

   A. "24 Hour 7 Day Service"
   B. "License # 4807"
   C. "Since 1935"
   D. "228-4495"

TEST 26

Read the following passage, and choose the best answer for each question.

The Yangtze River is not the longest, the widest, or the mightiest river in the world. But in one sense, it is the most important river, because it serves more people than any other. In every way the Yangtze is China's life stream.

The Yangtze isn't just a trade river, along which goods are picked up and distributed. It is an agricultural river, too. Networks of irrigation ditches stretch out from it to millions of farms. There people work endlessly, raising their family's food and the nation's food.

The Yangtze River begins somewhere high in the area north of Tibet, hurtling down from a three-mile height. It surges for hundreds of miles, roars through canyons, and picks up branches. Only in the last 1,000 miles of its 3,200-mile journey does the Yangtze become China's blessing.

   1. The Yangtze River begins its journey somewhere in the
      ————— part of Tibet.

    A. central   B. south   C. north   D. eastern

   2. How many miles does the river travel?
    A. One thousand miles.
    B. Thirty-two hundred miles.
    C. Thirty-two thousand miles.
    D. Hundreds of miles.

3. The upper part of the Yangtze River ——————

    A. flows through wide plains.
    B. rushes down from high mountains.
    C. is good for navigation.
    D. is more valuable than the lower part.

4. The Yangtze River is ——————

    A. primarily a trade river.
    B. not only a trade but an agricultural river.
    C. a famous river mainly because it surges for hundreds
       of miles.
    D. not the longest river in the world, but the widest
       and mightiest one.

5. From this article we have learned that ——————

    A. millions of farms along the river are often flooded.
    B. a dam should be built to hold back the waters in the
       upper part of the river.
    C. the nation's food depends only on the Yangtze River.
    D. The Yangtze River is China's source of strength.

TEST 27

Read the following passage, and choose the best answer for each question.

The hamburger is one of the most popular foods in the country. Americans eat about forty billion of them a year.

Charles Kuralt, of CBS-TV News, started keeping an <u>account</u> of the various names for the different kinds and sizes of burgers around the country. He found king burgers, queen burgers, mini burgers, maxi burgers, tuna burgers, poppa burgers, momma burgers, and baby burgers. In the South, he ate Dixie burgers, and in Washington, D.C., he ate Capitol burgers. Some restaurant owners named burgers after themselves: Buddy burgers, Cluck burgers, Juan burgers, and dozens more.

No matter what they're called, Americans eat a lot of them!

1. The best title is —————
   A. A Man Who Loves Hamburgers.
   B. Many Kinds of Burgers.
   C. American Foods.
   D. Eating in America.

2. In the South, Charles ate —————
   A. Capitol burgers.   B. poppa burgers.
   C. Dixie burgers.   D. Buddy burgers.

3. Americans eat about forty billion hamburgers each ————
  A. year.   B. week.
  C. day.   D. month.

4. One kind of burger not mentioned in the story is the
  ————
  A. tuna burger.   B. Jake burger.
  C. maxi burger.   D. Dixie burger.

5. The underlined word "account" means ————
  A. recipe.   B. record.
  C. diary.   D. column.

TEST 28

Read the following passage, and choose the best answer for each question.

Basketball is one sport — perhaps the only sport — whose exact origin can safely be stated. During the winter of 1891-1892, Dr. James Naismith, a college instructor in Springfield, Massachusetts, invented the game of basketball in order to provide exercise for the students between the closing of the football season and the opening of the baseball season. He attached fruit baskets overhead on the walls at two ends of the gymnasium, and, using a soccer ball, organized nine-man teams to play his new game in which the purpose was to toss the ball into one basket and to keep the opposing team from tossing the ball into the other basket. Although there have since been many changes in the rules, the game is basically the same today.

1. When was basketball invented?
    A. Earlier than football.
    B. Later than football.
    C. At the same time as football.
    D. The exact origin was not known.

2. How many members were there on the first basketball team?
    A. Five.   B. Nine.
    C. Ten.   D. Indefinite.

3. Basketball was invented because _____

    A. students needed winter exercise.

    B. students were tired of playing football and baseball.

    C. it could be played indoors.

    D Dr. Naismith thought it was more fun than other games.

4. Where was the first basketball game played?

    A. On a university football field.

    B. On a farm.

    C. In a gym.

    D. In Dr. Naismith's yard.

5. What equipment was used in the first basketball game?

    A. Fruit baskets and a soccer ball.

    B. A basketball and a gymnasium.

    C. A gymnasium and fruit baskets.

    D. No special equipment was used.

TEST 29

Read the following passage, and choose the best answer for each question.

The children were working hard at their desks when a big truck stopped outside the village school. Two smiling young women and one man got out of the truck. The children knew one of the women. She lived in the village, and sometimes came to school to examine them for signs of illness. The man carried something in his hand called a spray gun. The children knew what it was and knew what to do. Quickly they ran outside, lined up and knelt on the ground before the man. Some thought it was great fun and laughed and shouted. Some were afraid and cried. But everyone got well dusted with spray powder before the truck moved on. In other villages, there were other trucks stopping at one house after another. The walls in every house were sprayed.

1. Why did the people in that village take the spray?
    A. for fun
    B. to kill insects
    C. to prevent disease
    D. to protect the people in the truck

2. How many people came to the village to spray the inhabitants?
    A. 1   B. 2
    C. 3   D. 4

3. Which of the following statements is true?

   A. The children had never been treated this way before.

   B. The children had been sprayed many times and knew it would be painful.

   C. The children had never been sprayed before, so many of them were scared.

   D. The children had been sprayed before, and some of them liked it.

4. Which of the following describes the people in the truck?

   A. They were threatening.

   B. They were friendly.

   C. They were attractive.

   D. They were unhealthy.

5. What did the children do when they saw the truck?

   A. They took their medicine.

   B. They knelt under their desks.

   C. They ran out of the classroom.

   D. They showed respect to the man because he was a great doctor.

TEST 30

Read the following passage, and choose the best answer for each question.

Instructions for the Use of Your New Hercules Vacuum Cleaner

1. Do not oil. The motors are permanently lubricated.

2. Do not operate cleaner without dust bag.

3. Disconnect power cord from electrical outlet before changing bags.

4. Do not run cleaner over power cord.

5. Avoid picking up hard objects with your cleaner to prevent bag breakage, hose clogging, or motor damage.

6. Warning: Electric shock could occur if used outdoors or on wet surfaces.

---

1. According to the directions, where or when is it dangerous to use this cleaner?

    A. Outdoors.

    B. Indoors.

    C. When it is disconnected.

    D. When it has not been lubricated.

2. Using this cleaner on a wet surface may cause _____

    A. the hose to clog.   B. the bag to break.

    C. electric shock.   D. oil leakage.

3. Which of the following will NOT damage the cleaner?

    A. Picking up nails with it.
    B. Clogging the hose.
    C. Running over its power cord.
    D. Using a dust bag.

4. How often should you oil the cleaner?

    A. Once every use.
    B. Once every three months.
    C. Once a year.
    D. Never.

5. What should you not use your vacuum cleaner to clean?

    A. Hair.   B. Soil.
    C. Coins.   D. Dust.

TEST 31

Read the following passage, and choose the best answer for each question.

Did you know that a change in the weather can affect your behavior? For example, a Japanese scientist studied the number of packages and umbrellas left behind on buses and streetcars in Tokyo. He found that passengers were most forgetful on days when the barometer fell. Also, after studying patterns of car accidents in Ontario, the Canadians found that most accidents took place when the barometer fell. Other studies show that a sudden rise in temperature within a low-pressure area can lead to destructive acts, including suicide.

1. According to this passage, a change in the weather ⎯⎯⎯⎯⎯⎯

    A. is caused by the behavior of people.
    B. affects the way people behave.
    C. affects personal behavior only in Tokyo.
    D. affects only those who ride buses and streetcars.

2. When the barometer fell in Tokyo ⎯⎯⎯⎯⎯⎯
    A. hundreds of people were injured by the falling debris.
    B. people's memories improved.
    C. people always brought umbrellas with them when they went out.
    D. people tended to forget things on public transportation.

3. The studies mentioned in this passage show that changes in the weather produce all but which of the following?

    A. temporary forgetfulness
    B. a lack of coordination in car drivers
    C. a reduction of pressure at work
    D. suicides

4. It can be inferred that when the barometer rises —————

    A. more people will commit suicide.
    B. people will be able to concentrate better.
    C. people will suffer less pressure.
    D. people will not drive as much.

5. What is Ontario?

    A. It is a research institute.
    B. It is a barometer.
    C. It is a city.
    D. It is a Canadian province.

TEST 32

Read the following passage, and choose the best answer for each question.

The monster came toward us with twice our speed. We gasped in amazement. We were awed and silent. The animal came on, playing with the waves. It circled the Abraham Lincoln, then moved away two or three miles, leaving a bright wake. All at once it rushed from the dark horizon toward the ship with a frightening speed. When it was about twenty feet away, the light suddenly went out, and then appeared on the other side of us, as if the monster had gone beneath us.

1. In the above paragraph, what do you think the monster probably is?
   A. a ship   B. a whale
   C. an elephant   D. a giant wave

2. What does the name Abraham Lincoln stand for in this paragraph?
   A. an animal   B. a big fish
   C. a ship   D. a famous person

3. What is a wake?
   A. It is a kind of light.
   B. It is a path in the water.
   C. It is a tail.
   D. It is a monster.

4. How did the people feel?

    A. They were overjoyed.

    B. They were relaxed.

    C. They were astounded.

    D. They were aggressive.

5. At what time of day does this event take place?

    A. It is midday.

    B. It is morning.

    C. It is night.

    D. We cannot tell from the passage.

TEST 33

Read the following passage, and choose the best answer for each question.

Jones College is a large school which not only boasts a beautiful campus, but is also surrounded by charming rural villages. It offers advantages, such as small classes, individual counseling and private dorm rooms, which few schools of its size can match. The college offers degrees in a wide range of liberal arts fields, though no longer in oriental languages, and has a wide-ranging sports program embracing most of the usual collegiate sports, with the exception of football. In contrast to nearby White College, which requires students to live off-campus, Jones houses all of its all-male student population in dormitories on campus.

1. Students at Jones College _____
    A. enjoy fewer advantages than students at White College.
    B. must live in the nearby towns.
    C. do not know their classmates at all.
    D. cannot learn Japanese at school.

2. Students at Jones College _____
    A. love to play football.
    B. cannot be women.
    C. do not have a chance to study anything except science.
    D. must have at least one roommate.

3. Jones College has ――――――

    A. limits on the size of classes.

    B. few dormitories.

    C. few student services for a large school.

    D. many students studying in scientific fields.

4. What is true about Jones College?

    A. It is far away from White College.

    B. It is the number one football rival of White College.

    C. It has extensive university housing.

    D. Its students are all women.

5. At Jones College students ――――――

    A. must have a roommate.

    B. must play football.

    C. may live in a charming rural village.

    D. may study French.

TEST 34

Read the following passage, and choose the best answer for each question.

San Francisco is one of the most beautiful and unusual cities in the world, and it attracts a lot of tourists, both American and foreign, all year round. This fascinating town at the tip of the Californian peninsula is the western gateway of America. Historians call it "the city of the Golden Gate." Lovers call it "the city by the bay." Those who don't live there call it "Frisco." About one million people call it home. It was not until 1849 when the gold rush started in California that the town really began to grow. In fact, a year later, it became an incorporated city. The gold rush turned San Francisco into a boom town and established the basis for the city's later development into a major financial and cultural complex of America.

1. Without the gold rush, San Francisco would probably _____

   A. never have existed.
   B. be able to attract more tourists today.
   C. not have prospered as it did.
   D. have become the capital of the United States.

2. Tourists visit "the city of the Golden Gate" in _____
   A. spring.
   B. summer.
   C. autumn.
   D. every season of the year.

3. San Francisco has a population of about ———————

   A. one and a half million.

   B   one million.

   C. two million.

   D. fifty hundred thousand.

4. "The western gateway of America" refers to ———————

   A. San Francisco.   B. Los Angeles.

   C. California.   D. Seattle.

5. San Francisco became an incorporated city in ———————

   A. 1850.   B. 1849.

   C. 1847.   D. 1851.

TEST 35

Refer to the following newspaper classified advertising index:

Auction	11
Automotive	13-14
Business Opportunities	17-18
Capital to Invest	19-20
Mortgages	16
Real Estate	15

1. On which of the pages of the newspaper would one look to find the information on car sales?

   A. 11.   B. 13-14.
   C. 16.   D. 17-18.

2. Which of the following pages would most likely contain a list of homes for sale?

   A. 11.   B. 15.
   C. 16.   D. 19.

3. On which of the pages would one find the information on purchasing a convertible or limousine?

   A. 11.   B. 13-14.
   C. 16.   D. 17-18.

4. Under which designation would one find information on loans?

    A. Auction.
    B. Business Opportunities.
    C. Real Estate.
    D. Mortgages.

5. On which page should you begin your research if you want to start your own business?

    A. Auction.
    B. Business Opportunities.
    C. Real Estate.
    D. Mortgages.

TEST 36

Read the following passage, and choose the best answer for each question.

To the curious and the courageous, the sea still presents the challenge of the unknown, for ignorance is still the distinguishing characteristic of man's relation to the sea. But now, more than ever, necessity goads us onward in our exploration of the sea. We now have submarines, capable of steady submergence for many months, holding missiles capable of destruction many times greater than those used in World War II. For strategic reasons, therefore, we need urgently to learn more about the ocean bottom. Quite apart from the threat of war, another necessity pressed us to learn to master the sea. The necessity is basic to life itself: food. The lives of two thirds of the world's people are wholly dictated by that basic necessity; they are oppressed by hunger and by the weakness and disease which hunger generates. Out of the sea we can extract the food to relieve the hunger of these millions of people and give dignity to their lives. We must turn to the sea, because the bounty of the land has limits.

1. Apart from strategic considerations, we need to conquer the sea to solve the problem of ＿＿＿＿＿＿
    A. food supply.
    B. population explosion.
    C. environmental pollution.
    D. wildlife conservation.

2. Which of the following statements is true?

   A. The whole world population is suffering from hunger.
   B. The greatest waste in food consumption is brought about by the creatures from the ocean.
   C. Conquering the sea may ultimately mean the conquest of the world which has always been man's sole ambition.
   D. The ocean may hold the key to solving the world's food problem.

3. Wisely explored and fairly distributed of its harvests, the sea stands for _____

   A. a mighty threat.
   B. an unseen enemy.
   C. a great challenge.
   D. a potential promise.

4. According to the passage, which of the following statements is true?

   A. The sea presents few difficulties to man.
   B. The average man can read the sea like a map.
   C. As yet, we don't know well enough about the sea.
   D. It is only the curious and the courageous that reject taking up the challenge of exploring the sea.

5. Modern submarines can _____

   A. destroy all the natural resources at the ocean bottom.
   B. stay under water for months without returning to their base for supplies.
   C. be the one and only answer to win the next war.
   D. be economically used as transport vessels to ferry enormous quantities of strategic metals mined from the ocean floor.

TEST 37

Read the following passage, and choose the best answer for each question.

A new project is being set up to discover the best ways of sorting and separating garbage. When this project is complete, garbage will be processed like this: first, it will pass through sharp metal spikes which will tear open the plastic bags in which garbage is usually packed; then it will pass through a powerful fan to separate the lightest elements from the heavy solids; after that crushers and rollers will break up everything that can be broken. Finally, the garbage will pass under magnets, which will remove the bits of iron and steel; the rubber and plastic will then be sorted out in the final stage.

The first full-scale giant recycling plants are, perhaps, years away. But in some big industrial areas, where garbage has been dumped for so long that there are no holes left to fill up with garbage, these new automatic recycling plants may be built sooner. Indeed, with the growing cost of transporting garbage to more distant dumps, some big cities will be forced to build their own recycling plants before long.

1. When this project is complete, plants will be built for _____
   A. storing garbage.
   B. dumping garbage.
   C. the petrochemical industries.
   D. the recycling of waste.

2. Then, because everything which goes into the garbage can would be made into something useful, the word garbage could _____

    A. last forever.   B. revive.
    C. lose its meaning.   D. come back to life.

3. Crushers and rollers are used to _____

    A. separate the light elements.
    B. reduce items to small pieces.
    C. tear open the plastic bags.
    D. remove the sharp metal spikes.

4. The full-scale giant plants could not be built perhaps until many years later, but the big cities may speed up the projects out of _____

    A. money.   B. necessaries.
    C. necessity.   D. curiosity.

5. Among the problems big cities face, an essential one is that _____

    A. there are too many holes.
    B. there is an acute labor shortage.
    C. moving garbage to faraway dumps is too costly.
    D. finding the right man for the right job is difficult.

TEST 38

Read the following passage, and choose the best answer for each question.

The most exciting question of all is, does life exist beyond the earth? In recent years the trend has been toward the hypothesis that life is probably a normal phenomenon wherever the conditions are right, with the added qualification that proper conditions are not necessarily only those of the earth. It was long held, for example, that life on the planet Jupiter is impossible because of its extreme cold, crushing gravity and poisonous atmosphere. But there is evidence that the giant planet is warmer below the outer, cold layers than was first thought. The combination of gases in its atmosphere could produce organic or preorganic molecules. Since no one really knows all combinations of conditions under which life can evolve, it is best to be conservative about denying the existence of life on any planet.

1. Life on the planet Jupiter is a possibility which ――――――
   A. does not exist.
   B. should not be ruled out.
   C. excites all scientists.
   D. has never been explored.

2. Since we do not know all combinations of conditions under which life can develop, it is safer, the author advises, ——————

    A. to be conservative in asserting the existence of extraterrestrial life.
    B. to take an aggressive attitude in denying the existence of life in space.
    C. not to be too rash in dismissing the existence of life beyond the earth.
    D. not to express one's opinion too clearly.

3. Life on other planets is possible ——————

    A. when life-evolving conditions exist.
    B. only when their conditions match those of the earth.
    C. when the temperature is neither too hot nor too cold.
    D. when the atmosphere is not too dry.

4. According to the author, whether there is life beyond the earth is ——————

    A. the only question that excites people.
    B. one of several questions which excite people.
    C. one of the most exciting questions.
    D. the question which excites people the most.

5. When we add qualifications to a condition, we ——————

    A. give a higher quality to the condition.
    B. restrict and limit the condition.
    C. remove all restrictions on condition.
    D. enlarge the applicability of the condition.

TEST 39

Read the following passage, and choose the best answer for each question.

Reading is like riding a bicycle. You don't read everything at the same speed. How fast you read often depends upon your reason for reading. Sometimes you need to read slowly and carefully. You do this when you study. You also read slowly when you are following a set of directions.

Sometimes you don't want to read a whole article or story. You may just be looking for a fact you need to know. Or you might be looking for the answer to a question. When you read very quickly for such a purpose, you are skimming. The article you are reading may have subheads or less important titles. You can use these to help you find the part of the article you want.

Other times you may be reading for fun. You read most fiction this way. You don't have to remember facts or ideas, so you read fairly quickly. You often need to read such stories only once.

1. This article compares reading to riding a bicycle because
   _____

   A. reading is as much a pleasure as riding a bicycle.
   B. you vary speeds in reading as well as in riding a bicycle.
   C. you should read as fast as you ride a bicycle.
   D. you must read slowly as you ride a bicycle slowly for safety.

2. You skim when you ——————

    A. don't want to know all the details of a whole article or story.
    B. are following a set of directions.
    C. are studying for exams.
    D. ignore the subheads of an article.

3. When you read stories for fun, you generally read them ——————

    A. very carefully.
    B. many times.
    C. rather slowly.
    D. no more than one time.

4. Which of the following is one way of skimming?

    A. Reading carefully.
    B. Reading slowly.
    C. Memorizing something.
    D. Reading subheads.

5. When you read fiction for fun, you should ——————

    A. skim because the details are not important anyway.
    B. read carefully because many things in fiction are not true.
    C. read quickly because it is not necessary to remember the details.
    D. read it quickly so that you only have to read it once.

TEST 40

Read the following passage, and choose the best answer for each question.

OFFICE SPACE AVAILABLE

We have for lease carpeted, air-conditioned offices on the third floor of the Post-Intelligencer Building. Some offices with window views, all ready for immediate occupancy.

All utilities furnished, including janitor service and nightly / weekend security service.

Also includes parking, cafeteria, conference facilities, two passenger elevators and a freight elevator.

Building is within easy walking distance of stores, restaurants, bus service, Seattle City Center, and has easy access to the freeway.

For further information call Gary Walden at 628-8097.

---

1. The offices in the advertisement are for _____
   A. sale.   B. mortgage.
   C. rent.   D. auction.

2. All the offices advertised on the third floor of the Post-Intelligencer Building have _____
   A. window views.
   B. their own elevators.
   C. carpet and air conditioning.
   D. 24-hour security.

3. The Post-Intelligencer Building has a —————
   A. restaurant.   B. store.
   C. cafeteria.   D. resident security guard.

4. The Seattle City Center is —————
   A. close by.
   B. next door.
   C. near the freeway.
   D. a long distance from the Post-Intelligencer Building.

5. People who wish to lease office space in the Post-
   Intelligencer Building must —————
   A. supply their own security service.
   B. visit Gary Walden.
   C. wish to use conference facilities.
   D. call 628-8097.

TEST 41

Read the following passage, and choose the best answer for each question.

"Memorize these words." "Learn this spelling rule." "Don't forget the quiz tomorrow." You remember things every day, but how do you do it?

You find a telephone number in the phone book, dial it, and then forget it. This is your short-term memory. It lasts less than 30 seconds. However, you don't look in the phone book for a friend's number. You know it. This is your long-term memory. Your long-term memory has everything that you remember.

Why do you forget something ? You did not learn it in the beginning. This is the major reason for forgetting. For example, you meet some new people, and you forget their names. You hear the names, but you do not learn them. Then you forget them.

1. Your short-term memory helps you —————
   A. memorize new words you find in your reading materials.
   B. remember a phone number for a little while.
   C. spell English words correctly.
   D. prepare for a test.

2. Your long-term memory enables you to —————
   A. remember everything you come across every day.
   B. remember things for no more than 30 seconds.
   C. remember things every day and forget most of them.
   D. remember your friend's phone number for a long time.

3. We tend to forget the names of the new people we have just met because —————

    A. we did not try to memorize their names.
    B. we did not hear their names clearly.
    C. we have poor memories.
    D. we didn't have time to memorize their names.

4. What is long-term memory?

    A. Everything you learn.
    B. All the names and phone numbers you know.
    C. Things that take you a long time to remember.
    D. Anything that you remember.

5. According to the author, how long does short-term memory last?

    A. Until the next quiz.
    B. Until you really learn something.
    C. Less than half a minute.
    D. As long as it takes to dial a phone number.

TEST 42

Read the following passage, and choose the best answer for each question.

Elephants are the largest land mammals in the world. They live on two continents, Africa and southern Asia. Asian elephants, also known as Indian elephants, are easier to tame than African elephants and have been domesticated for 4000 years. The elephants you see in the circuses and zoos are nearly always Asian. African elephants are larger and have great ears like fans. Both the African and Indian elephants have strong, tough skin and long, lovely tusks. That is their problem. Elephants are in danger. People kill these animals in order to use their skin and their tusks. Because of the massive killings, elephants are dwindling in number and it is feared that by the end of the century, these huge mammals may be extinct. However, elephants are problems in some parts of Africa. In areas where the largest herds exist, they have become giant pests to the farmers. No fence is strong enough to keep these monsters away from the crops. Elephants go where they wish, destroying food crops and farm buildings. African farmers wonder if they can allow the elephants to continue to exist in their neighborhood.

1. In a zoo, one will most likely see an Asian elephant because
   _____

   A. Asian elephants can survive in a human environment.
   B. Asian elephants are smarter than African elephants.
   C. Asian elephants are easier to train than African elephants.
   D. Asian elephants are more destructive than African elephants.

2. Based on the passage, elephants are killed because

   _____

   A. they are pests to farmers.
   B. they destroyed food crops and buildings.
   C. they compete with humans for food and water.
   D. their tusks and skin are valuable.

3. Which of the following statements is NOT true?
   A. Elephants are the largest mammals in the world.
   B. African elephants are larger than Asian elephants.
   C. African elephants have created some problems for humans.
   D. Elephants live on two continents, Africa and southern Asia.

4. The reason why elephants may become extinct by the end of the century is _____
   A. that they have been domesticated by human beings.
   B. that they are hunted by human beings.
   C. that they are multiplying too fast.
   D. that they are major pests to farmers.

5. Which of the following is NOT true of Asian elephants?
   A. They are in danger.
   B. They are not as large as African elephants.
   C. They are killed for their valuable tusks.
   D. Their skin is not as tough as that of African elephants.

TEST 43

Read the following passage, and choose the best answer for each question.

Last spring my wife suggested that I call in a man to look at our lawnmower. It had broken down the previous summer, and though I promised to repair it, I had never got round to it. I would not hear of the suggestion and said that I would fix it myself. One Saturday afternoon, I hauled the machine into the garden and had a close look at it. As far as I could see, it only needed a minor adjustment: a turn of a screw here, a little tightening up there, a drop of oil and it would be as good as new. Inevitably, the repair job was not quite so simple. The mower firmly refused to mow, so I decided to dismantle it. The garden was soon littered with chunks of metal which had once made up a lawnmower. But I was extremely pleased with myself. I had traced the cause of the trouble. One of the links in the chain that drives the wheels had snapped. After buying a new chain I was faced with the insurmountable task of putting the confusing jigsaw puzzle together again. I was not surprised to find that the machine still refuse to work after I had reassembled it, for the simple reason that I was left with several curiously shaped bits of metal which did not seem to fit anywhere. I gave up in despair.

1. When the lawnmower broke down last summer, the writer _____

    A. immediately attempted to fix it.
    B. agreed to call in a repairman to take a look at it.
    C. promised to repair it himself.
    D. refused to have anything to do with it.

2. After a preliminary inspection of the mower, the writer concluded that _____

    A. the machine needed a complete overhaul.

    B. there was nothing seriously wrong.

    C. the job needed professional attention.

    D. it would be foolish for him to try the repair work.

3. The writer started to take the lawnmower apart _____

    A. the moment he laid his hands on the machine.

    B. because he was prompted by encouragement from his wife.

    C. for he deemed it impossible to spot the trouble without being told where it was.

    D. only after he had failed at his first attempt.

4. The cause which brought about all this trouble was finally discovered to be _____

    A. some missing screws.

    B. a few curiously shaped pieces of metal.

    C. want of lubricant.

    D. a broken piece in the driving chain.

5. To the writer, the whole experience was one of _____

    A. exasperation.

    B. exhilaration.

    C. accomplishment.

    D. exultation.

TEST 44

Read the following passage, and choose the best answer for each question.

It is a matter of common observation that although money incomes keep going up over the years, we never seem to become much better off. Prices are rising continuously. This condition is termed one of inflation; the money supply is becoming inflated so that each unit of it becomes less valuable. We have grown accustomed in recent years to higher and higher rates of inflation. What could be bought ten years ago for one dollar now costs well over two dollars. Present indications are that this rate of inflation is tending to rise rather than to fall. If in the real world, our money incomes go up at the same rate as prices, one might think that inflation does not matter. But it does. When money is losing its value, it lacks one of the qualities of a good money — stability of value. It is no longer acceptable as a store of value; and it becomes an unsuitable standard of deferred payments. Nobody wants to hold a wasting asset, so people try to get rid of money as quickly as possible. Inflation therefore stimulates consumer spending, and deters saving.

1. Over the years, our incomes have been increasing, and we _____
   A. seem to prosper at a quicker rate.
   B. are actually no better, if not worse, in our financial condition.
   C. can afford to buy more of the things that we want.
   D. have managed to keep prices down.

2. Inflation is a situation in which ——————

   A. we can watch our money increase in its value.

   B. unemployment is no longer a problem.

   C. people can always find better paying jobs.

   D. money keeps losing its value.

3. If incomes and prices rise together, so the writer argues, ——————

   A. there will be no more market fluctuations.

   B. money will hold its value.

   C. inflation will remain to be a problem.

   D. inflation poses no problem.

4. When money loses its value, ——————

   A. it is no longer stable.

   B. its rate against gold will be kept at the same level.

   C. goods will lose their value, thus creating no new problems.

   D. incomes will keep stable to lessen the problems of inflation.

5. In a period of inflation, people are likely to ——————

   A. invest heavily on the stock market.

   B. save money.

   C. hold on to money as a dependable asset.

   D. spend money and not bother to save.

TEST 45

Read the following passage, and choose the best answer for each question.

COMMUTER BUS SERVICE
New York City — Brennan, N.J.
(Effective Sept. 1998 – May 1999)

SCHEDULE

- Buses leave Port Authority Bus Terminal, New York City, from 7:00 a.m., and every half-hour thereafter, until 11:30 p.m. (7 days a week)

- Buses leave Brennan station 20 minutes before and after every hour from 6:20 a.m. until 10:40 p.m. (7 days a week)

- Evening rush hours (5:00 p.m. to 7:00 p.m.) : buses leave Port Authority Terminal every 15 minutes (Monday-Friday)

- Holidays: buses leave every hour on the hour, each direction (Trip time: 30 minutes each way)

TICKETS

- One way: $ 1.50   • Commuter ticket (10 trips) : $ 10.00

- All tickets must be purchased at Window 12, Port Authority Bus Terminal, or at the Brennan station window BEFORE boarding buses.

---

1. At which of the following times does a bus leave New York for Brennan on Tuesdays?

   A. 9:30 a.m.   B. 11:15 a.m.
   C. 2:45 p.m.   D. 10:20 p.m.

2. If you had to meet a friend at the bus station in Brennan at 10:15 a.m. on a Friday, which is the latest bus you could take from New York?

    A. The 10:00 a.m. bus.
    B. The 9:30 a.m. bus.
    C. The 9:00 a.m. bus.
    D. The 8:20 a.m. bus.

3. What time does a bus leave Brennan for New York City on Saturdays?

    A. 5:15 p.m.   B. 7:10 p.m.
    C. 9:40 p.m.   D. 11:40 p.m.

4. Where should passengers buy their tickets?

    A. From the driver before boarding the bus.
    B. From the driver after boarding the bus.
    C. At the door near this notice.
    D. At a terminal ticket window.

5. If you need to take a bus on Christmas Day, what time will the bus leave?

    A. 12:09 p.m.   B. 12:45 p.m.
    C. 12:30 p.m.   D. 1:00 p.m.

TEST 46

Read the following passage, and choose the best answer for each question.

The first bridges were pieces of wood that someone placed across a stream. These bridges were not very strong. If too many people tried to cross at one time the bridges broke. The people fell into the water! Later people made bridges of stone. The Romans made some very good bridges of stone and many of these are still standing today. Sometimes, however, no one could build a bridge across a river. The river was too wide and too deep and the water was too strong. If there was no bridge, the people had to use boats to cross it.

About two hundred years ago, a man named Darby built the first iron bridge. It crossed the River Severn in England. It was very strong and cars and trucks use it today. Bridge builders then began to use iron and steel to make two kinds of bridges. The first kind is the suspension bridge. "Suspension" means "hanging." There are usually two or more towers which hold up very strong cables. The ends of the cables are fastened at each side of the river. The bridge hangs down from the cables. The longest and most famous suspension bridge is the Golden Gate Bridge in San Francisco in the U.S. The other kind of steel bridge does not have cables. It is made in a number of different parts. Each readymade part is very strong and joins on to the next part. One example of this kind of bridge is the Kuan-tu Bridge across the Tam-sui River in the northern part of Taiwan.

1. The least durable bridges are made of _____
   A. wood.   B. stone.
   C. iron.   D. steel.

2. The Romans were very successful in building _____
   A. wooden bridges.   B. stone bridges.
   C. iron bridges.   D. steel bridges.

3. The first iron bridge built two hundred years ago _____
   A. has fallen apart.
   B. can still be seen in the United States.
   C. crosses the river Thames.
   D. can still be used by automobiles today.

4. The Kuan-tu Bridge of Taiwan _____
   A. was built in the same way as the Golden Gate Bridge.
   B. used a lot of cables.
   C. was constructed by joining the parts together.
   D. is the longest bridge of its kind.

5. The Golden Gate Bridge in San Francisco is famous for
   its _____
   A. towers.   B. length and structure.
   C. scenic views.   D. iron and steel.

TEST 47

Read the following passage, and choose the best answer for each question.

If there is any single factor that makes for success in living it is the ability to profit by defeat. Every success I know has been achieved because the person was able to analyze defeat and actually profit by it in his next undertaking. Confuse defeat with failure, and you are indeed doomed to failure, for it isn't defeat that makes you fail; it is your own refusal to see in defeat the guide and encouragement to success.

Defeats are nothing to be ashamed of. They are routine incidents in the life of every man who achieves success. But defeat is a dead loss unless you do face it without humiliation, analyze it and learn why you failed. Defeat, in other words, can help to cure its own cause. Not only does defeat prepare us for success, but nothing can arouse in us such a compelling desire to succeed. If you let a baby grasp a rod and try to pull it away he will cling more and more tightly until his whole weight is suspended. It is this same reaction which should give you new and greater strength every time you are defeated. If you exploit the power which defeat gives, you can accomplish with it far more than you are capable of when all is serene.

1. What does the author know?
    A. He knows at least several cases of success.
    B. He knows every success in life.
    C. He knows every success that has been achieved by man.
    D. He knows every success that a particular person achieved.

2. Defeat is valuable ——————
   A. because it forces you to face it without humiliation.
   B. in that it provides the guide and encouragement to success.
   C. because of your own refusal to see in it the guide and encouragement to success.
   D. since you refuse to see in it the guide and encouragement.

3. If you face defeat without humiliation, analyze it and learn why you failed, defeat ——————
   A. will become a dead loss.
   B. is nothing but a dead loss.
   C. is a dead loss according to the author.
   D. is anything but a dead loss.

4. The baby will cling more and more tightly ——————
   A. as soon as you let him grasp a rod.
   B. when you have pulled the rod away.
   C. if you try to pull away the rod from his grasp.
   D. unless you try to pull the rod away.

5. If you exploit the power which defeat gives, you can, according to the author, accomplish with it far more ——————
   A. than you have.
   B. than the baby.
   C. than your accomplishment.
   D. than when there has been no defeat.

TEST 48

Read the following passage, and choose the best answer for each question.

"You'd better pick up a few things on the way."

"What do we need?"

"Some roast beef, for one thing. I bought a quarter of a pound coming from my aunt's."

"Why a quarter of a pound, Joan?" said Rogin, deeply annoyed. "That's just about enough for one good sandwich."

"So you have to stop at a delicatessen. I had no more money."

He was about to ask, "What happened to the thirty dollars I gave you on Wednesday?" but he knew that would not be right.

"I had to give Phyllis money for the cleaning woman," said Joan.

Phyllis, Joan's cousin, was a young divorcee, extremely wealthy. The two women shared an apartment.

"Roast beef," he said, "and what else?"

"Some shampoo, sweetheart. We've used up all the shampoo. And hurry, darling, I've missed you all day."

"And I've missed you," said Rogin, but to tell the truth he had been worrying most of the time. He had a younger brother whom he was putting through college. Joan had debts he was helping her to pay, for she wasn't working. She was looking for something suitable to do.

1. The conversation in the passage probably took place _____
   A. over the telephone.   B. in Joan's apartment.
   C. in Rogin's imagination.   D. at a delicatessen.

2. One may go to a delicatessen _____
   A. to buy some roast beef.   B. to cash one's check.
   C. to cool down.   D. to buy some shampoo.

3. Joan explained to Rogin how she had spent the thirty dollars
   _____

   A. because Rogin insisted on knowing what had happened to it.
   B. when Rogin said the amount wasn't right.
   C. even though Rogin did not ask her to.
   D. because she wanted Rogin to blame Phyllis.

4. Which of the following statements about Phyllis is true?
   A. Though very rich, she cleaned the apartment to earn some
      extra money.
   B. She shared an apartment with Joan's cousin.
   C. She collected money from Joan, which she gave to the
      cleaning woman.
   D. Her husband was probably away on some business.

5. Which of the following statements about Rogin is true?
   A. He had been missing Joan all that day.
   B. His greatest concern at this moment was money.
   C. For financial reasons, he did not want his younger brother
      to get a college education.
   D. He is an extremely selfish person.

TEST 49

Read the following passage, and choose the best answer for each question.

One thing that startles visitors to London is the social status that animals enjoy there. Pet estimates indicate that there is at least one pet for every man, woman, and child in the city. Cats alone are estimated at five million. And to this figure must be added the dogs, birds, fish, ponies, rabbits, tortoises, monkeys, and other far more novel beasts which are privileged members of many a London household.

The most famous and favored of London's pets, however, do not share anyone's household. They have their own 34-acre estate in Regent's Park, the preserve of the Zoological Society of London since 1828. There are 7,000 of them, including the birds, beasts, and the 3,000 fish, and they are probably the most thoroughly observed, adored, and talked about animals alive. They are everyone's pets…or, at least, the pets of everyone who can squeeze in.

On a fine holiday afternoon 50,000 visitors may crowd into the London Zoo. In a year two million pay admission, about as many people as go to all of London's famous art galleries and museums. The feel of the place is evident on any sunny summer afternoon in the Children's Zoo, a special pets' corner. Here goats, ponies, donkeys, rabbits, lambs, parrots, pigeons, and even a reindeer and a baby elephant roam freely to kiss and to be kissed by tiny visitors. This special Children's Zoo was opened in 1935 to bring together zoo babies and London babies even more intimately than the larger enclosures would allow. Like many other Regent's Park "firsts," it has since been copied at zoos around the world.

1. Visitors to London are surprised that —————

    A. the favorite household pet is a cat.

    B. some Londoners keep rabbits and tortoises as household pets.

    C. some Londoners keep squirrels as household pets.

    D. animals enjoy social status.

2. There are as many pets in London as —————

    A. there are houses.

    B. there are inhabitants.

    C. there are families.

    D. there are privileged members.

3. "Tiny visitors" means —————

    A. children.   B. adults.

    C. grown-ups.   D. students.

4. The main idea in this selection is that —————

    A. the London Zoo occupies a 34-acre estate in Regent's Park.

    B. the inhabitants of London take great pride in their art galleries and museums.

    C. Londoners are fond of household pets and of animals in the zoo.

    D. London has a special zoo for children.

5. The best title for this selection is —————

    A. London's Household Pets.

    B. London's Famous Zoo.

    C. London's Famous Art Galleries.

    D. Zoo Babies and London Babies.

TEST 50

Refer to the following packaging label:

Servings per Package	4 —— one-cup size

Nutrition Information per Serving

Calories	120
Protein (grams)	1
Carbohydrate (grams)	25
Fat (grams)	1

Percentages of U.S. Recommended Daily Allowances (USRDA)

Protein	10
Vitamin A	4
Vitamin C	2
Thiamin	2
Riboflavin	15
Calcium	15
Niacin	**

** contains less than 2 % of USRDA

1. How many half-cup servings are there per package?

   A. 4   B. 8
   C. 120   D. 25

2. How many calories are there in two servings?

    A. 120   B. 60

    C. 240   D. 480

3. Which of the following nutrients is not found in appreciable amounts?

    A. vitamin C   B. vitamin A

    C. niacin   D. riboflavin

4. What do the letters RDA signify?

    A. Registered with the Department of Agriculture.

    B. Riboflavin, vitamin A and vitamin D.

    C. Redistribution Amounts.

    D. Recommended Daily Allowances.

5. If you want to regulate your calorie intake to about 2000 calories per day, how many packages could you eat in one day?

    A. 1   B. 4

    C. 15   D. 20

中級英語閱讀測驗（學生用書）

售價：120 元

主　　　編／劉　毅

發　行　所／學習出版有限公司　　☎ (02) 2704-5525

郵 撥 帳 號／ 05127272 學習出版社帳戶

登　記　證／局版台業 *2179* 號

印　刷　所／文聯彩色印刷有限公司

台 北 門 市／台北市許昌街 17 號 6F　　☎ (02) 2331-4060

台灣總經銷／紅螞蟻圖書有限公司　　☎ (02) 2795-3656

本公司網址／ www.learnbook.com.tw

電 子 郵 件／ learnbook@learnbook.com.tw

2020 年 7 月 1 日新修訂

4713269383765